Bamba Beach

PRATIMA MITCHELL
ILLUSTRATED BY DAVID DEAN

BLOOMSBURY EDUCATION
LONDON OXFORD NEW YORK NEW DELHI SYDNEY

BLOOMSBURY EDUCATION

Bloomsbury Publishing Plc
50 Bedford Square, London, WC1B 3DP, UK
29 Earlsfort Terrace, Dublin 2, Ireland

BLOOMSBURY, BLOOMSBURY EDUCATION and the Diana logo are trademarks of
Bloomsbury Publishing Plc

First published in Great Britain in 2009 by A & C Black, an imprint of Bloomsbury
Publishing Plc
This edition published in Great Britain in 2021 by Bloomsbury Publishing Plc

Text copyright © Pratima Mitchell, 2009
Illustrations copyright © David Dean, 2009

Pratima Mitchell and David Dean have asserted their rights under the Copyright, Designs
and Patents Act, 1988, to be identified as Author and Illustrator of this work

A catalogue record for this book is available from the British Library

ISBN: PB: 978-1-4729-8998-7; ePDF: 978-1-4729-9000-6; ePub: 978-1-4729-8999-4

2 4 6 8 10 9 7 5 3 1

Printed and bound in in the UK by CPI Group Ltd, CR0 4YY

To find out more about our authors and books visit www.bloomsbury.com and sign up
for our newsletters

CONTENTS

CHAPTER ONE

Hari lived in a fishing village in Bamba Beach. Bamba is a seaside village in Goa. The nearest town was many miles away, so he was a country boy – tough, wiry and used to a simple life.

Hari wasn't a person to blow his own conch shell, but he knew he was pretty good at a few things. By the age of eleven he could:

1. Swim quite far out to sea (breast stroke and a sort of crawl).

2. Climb a coconut tree (not too often, because the coconuts were reserved for someone else to harvest).

3. Do mental arithmetic (rupees 145,718 plus rupees 308,960 equals rupees 454,678).

4. Go fishing with his father and sort out mackerel from sprat, prawn, pomfret, kingfish, lobster, and so on. Mend nets.

5. Read and write very well in his own language, Konkani. He was top of his class at St Agnes Catholic School for Boys and Girls.

6. Speak English, as in "Good morning, sir/madam", "You want go in fishing boat?", "Goodbye, have-a-nice-day".

One hot November night, Hari woke up with a start and found a full moon staring boldly at his face. He rubbed his eyes. It seemed like the Man in the Moon was grinning down at him. Hari brushed away a mosquito that was nibbling his ear. The window was wide open. A delicious cool sea breeze drifted in, but so did a lot of other things – moths, flies, bluebottles and of course mosquitoes.

He got up and went to look outside. His gaze travelled from the ink-black shadows of coconut palms in the sandy yard to the line of silvery surf beyond the fence.

In the moonlight he saw the waves curling in and out. He imagined the sea creatures tumbling around in the dark-green waters – squid waving their tentacles, shoals of sprat, tiny crabs plopping and sucking down into the wet sand, plankton thicker than the Milky Way.

A few lights were winking far away on the horizon. They were the lights of fishing boats in the bay beside Bamba Beach.

From the next room, Hari heard the murmur of his parents' voices. They weren't asleep, either. He tried to eavesdrop.

"School fees… doctor's bill… thatch has to be repaired… boat needs new engine… grocer's bill… bills… bills…"

It was a list as long as a piece of rope. Hari was very aware that there was no money to pay for anything. The reason there was no money was because there were very few fish left in Bamba Bay. And the reason for *that* was because the bay had been hit very hard by the tsunami.

Even though the west coast of India had not been physically affected, the ocean currents had dramatically changed. The good fish, which sold quickly in the market, were now swimming much further out, way beyond the reach of Hari's father's old coconut-wood boat.

Now a steel-hulled boat with an outboard motor would be a different matter. *Then* he would be able to travel further out and lower his nets in the deep. The tourist hotels paid good money to feed the visitors who came to Goa. But no fish equalled no money. The arithmetic was as simple as that.

Hari rubbed his eyes again. Dawn was still a long way off. The coconut palms rustled their underskirts. A very early cock crowed and Hari saw a shadow flitting past in the next-door compound. Was it a stray dog or a ghost? Or was it the granny from next door, whom everyone in the village called the Witch?

Hari yawned an ear-splitting yawn and found his bed again. He and his sister Radha weren't allowed to talk to the Witch, or any of the Next Doors. They, like Hari's family, were fisherfolk, and village gossip whispered that the father was a bit of a bully. There were rumours that he shouted at his family when he got angry. But he was rich enough to own a fishing boat with an outboard motor.

Hari fell asleep and dreamed about the Witch. She flew up to a coconut tree and started to cackle. He woke up to find it was morning and the cock was crowing loudly in their back yard.

"Is it true," Hari asked his father as he ate his breakfast, "that the Witch has cast her spells on all the other fishermen in

Bamba Beach? Everyone is saying that nobody will ever bring in a catch to equal her son's. That no one will ever be as rich as him!"

"Tchh! Complete rubbish!" Hari's father replied. He believed that praying to Lord Krishna had more power than any bad magic. "But even so, I don't want my children mixing with the Next Doors."

"Why not?" asked Hari.

"It's to do with some old family quarrel," his mother explained. "You must respect Papa's wishes."

Hari heard Papa sigh. "It's no good being jealous of Next Door's wealth. What we need is capital."

"But, Papa, how can you get Delhi? It isn't possible," wondered seven-year-old Radha.

Hari laughed. "Stupid! Papa's not talking about the capital of *India*. Capital means money. You know – rupees, dollars, pounds, roubles!"

Radha was crushed. She was very proud of her GK, or general knowledge. On Wednesday evenings, she watched *Who'll Become a Millionaire?* on TV, and dreamed of winning the quiz one day. Her lip trembled.

Hari, who was very fond of his sister, immediately felt ashamed. He gave her a friendly push. "Come on. Race you to the creek!"

As they ran, their bare feet smacked the damp sand. At low tide, Bamba Beach was the best running track anywhere. Near the creek, where the small river met the sea, a pack of stray dogs was barking at the hermit crabs. The crabs ignored the strays and carried on scuttling onto the sand. Then a squabble of gulls appeared, so the dogs had something else to get excited about.

The sky was a perfect bright blue and the sea looked so inviting that Hari quickly stepped out of his shorts and ran into the water in his underpants. He swam strongly to the rocks. Then he turned over on his back, closing his eyes and letting the warm current carry him back to the shore.

Two tourists, a young man and a young woman, approached the creek. They had walked all the way from the neighbouring village. They came up to Hari's father's fishing boat, which lay on the sand. Radha was playing in the shade of the bow with some tiny blue and white shells.

Hari waded out of the water and went up to the tourists. He flashed a smile. "Good morning, sir, madam! Wanna go in gen-u-ine fishing boat? Round the bay trip is only rupees 80!"

Eighty rupees were worth less than one pound for the tourists. The trip took over an hour. Surely they would see what a bargain they were getting!

But the pair shook their heads.

Hari was disappointed. If lots of tourists came up to the creek and wanted fishing trips, then things would be very different. He knew that when demand was greater than supply, prices went up. If he could charge more, then he would start earning good money. Even if it took years, he would collect enough boat fares, get a loan from the bank and *then* they could buy the kind of boat they needed to catch fish in deep water.

But tourists seldom walked out so far. They preferred to lie on the sand close to their hotels and sunbathe, or splash about in the waves. They were frightened of the stray dogs, of being far from their base, and goodness knows what else.

Hari looked sadly at the pair, who had turned to go back. If only he could think of a way to earn some money! What was the use of coming top of his class if he couldn't help his father and mother?

Maybe he should leave school and sell fruit on the beach. Maybe he should look for work as a tea-shop assistant or washer-up. Maybe he should invent something so brilliant that the President of India would give him a gold medal.

Maybe he should save someone's life and get a reward.

There were so many possibilities. Though, sadly, he realised that none of them were likely to happen to him.

CHAPTER TWO

The Witch was called Amma by her three granddaughters, Tara, Anjali and Seema. She was very old, slightly bent, with a skinny frame and white hair pulled back in an untidy bun. She was getting forgetful and vague, but she couldn't understand why people in Bamba Beach had stopped speaking to her. What had she done wrong? Just given her son his inheritance *before* she passed away, so he could make good use of it.

Amma was the daughter of a fisherman, the widow of a fisherman and her only son,

Madhu, followed the same trade. Even his marriage had been arranged to a young woman from a fisherman's family. However, Madhu's wife didn't bring a lot of money in her dowry, and a dowry was one important way families could add to their wealth. In another family, a bride without a dowry would most certainly have suffered.

But Amma was different. Amma didn't even mind that Madhu's wife had given the family three daughters, and not even one son.

"A child is a child – God's gift to the family. Times are changing. Girls won't become fishermen, but they will do something better. My daughter-in-law has produced three healthy, beautiful girls."

So Amma gave her son everything that would have come to him after her death. It was an early inheritance and Madhu used the money well. It helped him to set up as a modern, go-ahead fisherman.

This was the main reason why Madhu's family became unpopular in the village of Bamba Beach. The other villagers were jealous. His mother's money and his good business sense had made him rich, even though his temper sometimes got the better of him.

Now, here he was, shouting at his middle daughter, Anjali.

"If you keep getting such low marks in your exams, I will pull you out of school! You can stay at home and help your mother chop vegetables and cook rice! Why are you so stupid? Don't you know that girls have to go out to work these days? If you can't learn to read and write, you'll never get on in life!"

Anjali was a clever girl, but she didn't like school. At St Agnes, her teachers thought she was lazy and didn't try hard enough. Anjali hated school so much that she wept in her pillow at night. She wished she could write her letters properly, not back to front. However, she could tell wonderful stories, all about ghosts and goblins and talking animals.

Every evening, before sundown, there was a ritual. Tara, Anjali and Seema smartened up. Tara, the eldest, patted Pond's talcum powder on her face because she was nearly eleven and wanted to look well groomed. Anjali and Seema combed and plaited their hair and washed their faces.

Holding hands with Amma, the four of them strolled the mile to the creek and back. The evening sun got redder and redder, and then suddenly it was gone, over the edge of the horizon. Then they walked home in the pearly evening light.

On the far side of the beach, they saw tourists buying pineapples from the village girls. Amma would keep her granddaughters at a safe distance and hurry on towards the creek.

"Chi-chi-chi! Those white people are nearly naked! Don't go so close! They are not decent!"

Seema, the youngest, had a question for Amma. It had been bothering her for a while.

"Why won't Radha Over There play with me? We could be best friends and have so much fun. Anjali doesn't like playing my games."

Amma shrugged and looked vaguely into the distance.

When Seema asked her mother the same question, she was told:

"I don't know, baby. Something to do with your great-grandfather taking a coconut that fell from Them Over There's tree. I really don't know. Our families haven't spoken for generations!"

"How stupid!" Seema said crossly. She had watched Radha over the dividing wall for years. They were the same age. Radha played with dolls, and the game Knuckles, using shells, just like she did. She liked drawing pictures in the sand with a stick, too. Why couldn't they be friends?

Tara poked her sister. "Nosy parker!" she said. "Why must you stare at the

Them Over There like a hungry beggar? Aren't we good enough for you?"

"Rude girl!" shouted Seema. "Say sorry or I'll tell Daddy!"

"Tell tale, tell tale!"

"Pig! Donkey! Owl!" Seema pinched Tara and went and told her troubles to Motu, their black cat.

Motu (which means 'fatty') was the sleekest cat in the village, and the cleverest. He got rid of rats and snarled at snakes; he hissed at spiders and scorpions and spat at any creature that dared to trespass. He was also very sensitive to when someone was feeling sad. He snuggled up to the unhappy person (usually it was Anjali) and put a white paw reassuringly on their knee, or thigh, or whichever part of their body was available.

In turn, he was fed juicy morsels of fish and he felt like the king of the castle. He walked around with his nose in the air and sunned himself on Them Over There's back porch as though he owned the place.

But, the very next evening, Motu disappeared.

When two days had passed, Seema became really worried that something terrible had happened. She missed tickling his tummy. She missed his deep purr. Most of all she missed talking in his ear. All her secrets were stored inside his head.

"He's dead," she told Amma. Amma stroked the child's hair and mumbled something like, "Cats have nine lives, so even if he *has* died he'll come back for his eight other lives!"

Everyone was secretly afraid that Motu had been bitten by a snake, or that he had come under the wheels of a country bus. They searched his favourite haunts like the tea shop, the bakery and near the creek, where he loved to spring on hermit crabs.

Seema and her sisters asked at the grocery shop, the bicycle hire and the tourist restaurants in the village, but no one had seen him. It was very unsettling and family life didn't feel normal any more.

On the third night, Seema went to bed with a heavy heart. She tossed and turned, but couldn't get to sleep because her thoughts kept returning to Motu. Once she thought she heard a far-away meowing, but it was very faint, and the rustling of the palms drowned out all other sounds, except for the waves crashing on the shore.

Next morning, very early, while everyone was queuing for their turn at the bath bucket under the yard tap, a shout came from the wall dividing their house from Them Over There.

No one had called to them from Hari's house in living memory.

"Hoi, hoi, anyone there? I have your cat!"

Seema dropped her toothbrush and was the first to rush over and grab Motu – still fat and sleek – over the wall from Hari's arms. Then she remembered she wasn't supposed to speak to Them Over There.

Hari saved her the trouble. "I found him early this morning. He was stuck up a coconut palm. Must have been hunting crows or something and got too scared to come down again, so I climbed up and got him. He's a bit thin, but OK I think." Hari turned and went back to his breakfast. He didn't want to be scolded for speaking to the enemy, either.

But something happened that morning that hadn't happened in many, many years. In the eyes of the three girls, Hari Them Over There was now a hero. Something was starting to change. Something had begun to melt. Something that had stayed frozen a long time between the two families was taking a new form.

CHAPTER THREE

"I've run out of rice." Hari and Radha's mother sounded sad. "Run along to the grocer and see if he'll let me have a kilo of the cheapest rice on credit. I'll pay him at the end of the month."

Hari had overheard his parents fretting about the grocer's bill. He knew there wasn't really enough money to pay it off. Papa had found a job as a labourer building the new road between Margao town and their village. He carried heavy loads of sand and stone all day, but most of the money he earned went to pay the interest on their loan.

The village banking system went like this: the grocer lent money to most of the villagers; but they had to pay him more on top of what they had borrowed. For example, Hari's parents had 200 rupees on credit for things they had bought. But, in fact, they would have to repay the grocer 220 rupees, because he added on ten per cent interest. The grocer became steadily richer by lending his money, while everyone who took loans from him got poorer. The more they borrowed, the more they had to pay him back!

Mother was also running out of oil, sugar, tea and dal. She was watering down the children's milk to make it go further. Every morning, she went out to forage in the small wood behind the village for wild spinach and other greens to eat with their dal and rice. The little fish that Hari's father caught before dawn was sold at the bus stop, where they fetched just a few rupees.

When they arrived at the shop, Hari couldn't meet the shopkeeper's eye. He mumbled his message and waited for an answer. There was a heavy silence. Hari half-listened to the voice on the radio that was chirping on about the latest Bollywood film.

"Hritesh and Dimple in brand-new drama! Great songs and dances…"

The grocer was a mean man. "Are we the State Bank of India? Have we got a storeroom full of rice and dal and God-knows-what to keep for everyone who wants credit?" He looked at his hands.

"Or maybe I myself have turned into solid gold. Yes, that's what has happened. I am a golden man. Tell your mother, sonny, this is the *very last time* I shall oblige her…" And, very deliberately and slowly, he weighed out a kilo of rice – the cheapest, most maggoty rice in the shop – and poured it into a newspaper cone. He tucked in the ends expertly and practically flung it at Hari.

"Tut! No need to be so nasty. Leave the child alone. It's not *his* fault," said the grocer's wife. "God knows his father works hard enough and doesn't touch a drop of liquor. Not like some I know," she added.

Radha was clinging to Hari's elbow with big, scared eyes. The grocer must be very rich. She'd never really taken in how many things he had in his shop. Different kinds of soap, hair oil, detergent, jars of bright sweets, Cadbury's chocolate, Coca-Cola, bread, biscuits, combs, hair clips, coloured transfers, packets of crisps, many kinds of dal, huge tins of flour... How could he buy so many things unless he possessed a fortune? Radha wondered.

"I think we should open a shop," she informed her mother when they arrived home with the maggoty rice. "The grocer is very, very rich. We could be rich as well. Mother, let's open a shop!"

Hari struck his forehead with the palm of his hand. "You are so stupid! You can't open a shop without capital. C-A-P-I-T-A-L! Got it?"

Hari was finding it more and more painful seeing his parents sink into despair. The radio wasn't turned on to save electricity.

There was no more laughter and singing. They all carried on with a certain grim determination, but where would it end? How would things ever improve? Would the ocean currents go back to the way they were? Would the fish return to swim in the bay of Bamba Beach? Would they get bus loads of foreign tourists with 80 rupees in their pockets, all making a beeline for Papa's old boat?

Something drastic needed to happen to help his family. But what?

Hari thought long and hard. Maybe Brother Angelo would help.

Brother Angelo was the head of St Agnes Catholic School for Boys and Girls. Many years before, nearly all the teachers in Goa had been Catholic priests from Portugal. For centuries, Goa had been a colony of Portugal. Now it was very much part of India; the teachers were all Indian, some priests and some ordinary Goans. Half Hari's village was Hindu, like his family, and half was Catholic.

Brother Angelo was always telling the children about love and kindness. He might be just the right person to talk to about Hari's family's problems.

Hari was right. The head teacher *was* a good man, but nearly everyone in the village had money problems. How many of them could he help?

Brother Angelo leaned back in his chair. Hari could see his own face and blue school shirt reflected in the glass doors of the bookcase in front of him. "My car needs to be washed twice a week. If you take on the job I will pay you ten rupees each time. And I will certainly pray for your family. Oh, and one other thing – we can arrange free milk for you and your sister. Go and see the school secretary and tell her I sent you."

Twenty rupees a week and free milk at break for himself and Radha – well, at least it was a start. Hari knew that the family needed much more than he could ever earn just by washing cars. But he thanked Brother Angelo politely.

Hari walked back home humming a tune. Some of his friends were playing cricket in the lane.

"Howzzat? Come on, Hari, play with us!" they roared.

So he stopped for a while and hit a few shots, including a six. He even bowled out

a boy. Then, when the ball flew over a wall
and broke a window, everyone scattered
and hid before they could be told off.

Hari passed Amma watering the pot
plants in Next Door's garden and the three
girls playing hopscotch in the red dust. His
thoughts continued to dwell on getting
hold of that large sum of money. If they
couldn't afford an outboard motor, maybe
they could open a little shop? He could see
himself minding a shop after school.

At bedtime, when he couldn't get to
sleep, Hari enjoyed himself by imagining
that he was stacking the shelves: toys for
the children of Bamba Beach, sweets of
course, in every shape and form, bread
and fresh fruit for the tourists, flip-flops,
sunglasses and hats for them, too. He
felt really excited! He would practise his

English on the customers. "Good morning, madam! Yes, sir! One minute, madam. Try this, good sir! Very cheap today, half price." (Yesterday's bananas went brown so quickly in the heat.) "Fine, fine. You like fresh papaya every day? No problem. I will order it for you, miss. Have-a-nice-day! Happy holidays!"

Glancing at the window, Hari saw a few stars pricking through the coconut leaves. Somewhere in the village a dog barked and barked. The cross-eyed goat bleated in the shed and a night bird cried out once or twice. Hari drew the cover over himself.

Outside, on the other side of the wall, Amma the Witch was stumbling around in the dark. She unlatched the gate to Next Door's back yard and walked towards the beach. She stood on the shore and watched the waves lit by the strange, magical gleam of phosphorus. In they came and out again. She mumbled to herself as she stood there for a long time, very old and frail, as light as a small scoop of sand.

CHAPTER FOUR

The Next Door sisters were squabbling, in their usual fashion. They would slip into one argument, which managed to join onto another without pause. It was like knitting a very long scarf that had been cast on knitting needles a long time ago; it never seemed to end.

This particular argument was about Motu, their fat cat. Which of them was supposed to be giving him his meals?

The girls were meant to take it in turns: Tara one week, Anjali one week and

Seema one week. Two good bowls of rice and fishy bits and a saucer of fresh milk, with a bowl of water to be kept topped up.

"It's your turn."

"No, it's yours!"

"You never did clean out his dish."

"Yes, I did."

Somehow the argument changed to crayons. Why had Anjali grabbed all the best colours?

By the time that subject was exhausted, Anjali was pushing Seema off the table in the veranda.

"I have to do my homework. Go and do your colouring somewhere else."

Seema wouldn't move, so Anjali pulled her hair. Seema screamed. Their father was mending a fishing net in the yard.

He came and gave Anjali a look. His face was as dark as thunderclouds, when she burst into tears.

So Amma arrived to comfort her.

"Let her cry," Madhu shouted. "Don't interfere please, Amma." Then Amma turned away in a huff, like people who have been rebuffed do, so then the girls' mother had to comfort *her*.

It was quite a to-do. Seema picked up Motu and ran to the dividing wall between their house. She rested the cat on the grey stone and cuddled his smooth, well-fed body until he protested and jumped down to the other side. Motu trotted to Them Over There's back door. He entered in a lordly way without a backward glance. Obviously, he was quite at home there.

Seema watched Hari come out of the kitchen. He was leaving for the parish house at St Agnes to wash Brother Angelo's car.

When he saw Seema, he hesitated. All the neighbours had heard the commotion at Next Door's. He lifted one eyebrow and spoke. "What's up? Everyone in your house is crying!"

Seema was taken by surprise. She knew she shouldn't be speaking to Hari, but she was still upset, and the words tumbled out before she could stop them. "It's all Anjali's fault – she can't do her homework so she gets angry with everyone."

"Why can't she do it?" asked Hari. "What's the problem?"

Seema stamped her foot. "It's because she finds it hard to read, and her writing's all funny and backwards. But she's really very clever and tells amazing stories. Shall I tell you the one about the ghost in the guava tree?"

Hari smiled. "Not right now. I have to wash Father Angelo's car before he goes to a meeting in Margao."

"Why do you have to do that?"

"Because he's paying me ten rupees a wash and my family needs the money."

Seema sucked her finger. She was still quite babyish, even though she was seven. She filed away the information Hari had given her, and later in the evening she reported it to her mother.

"The boy said they have no money."

"You mean you've been talking to Them Over There?"

"He rescued Motu…"

"There's no need to get too friendly with them."

"I've told you before, mind your own business," scolded Tara.

And that started *another* fight, which went on until Madhu came home to eat his dinner. He growled at the girls to behave and then took the boat out to sea. It was high tide and there was bound to be a very good catch. A very good catch meant lots of money. At least the Next Doors didn't have to worry about *that*.

After they had eaten, the three girls sat under the light in the front room to do their homework. They were still squabbling.

Anjali pushed Tara's elbow because she was taking up too much space on the table. Seema kicked Anjali by accident, so she got a glare. Tara told Anjali to zip her mouth, because she kept sighing and asking for help with her writing.

"If you talk one more time, you'll be really sorry for yourself," Tara warned. Tara had a line in twisty bangles – a form of torture in which she twisted the skin on Anjali's wrist until it hurt.

Anjali jumped up and ran outside crying. She was supposed to be writing a story and she felt sure it was full of spelling mistakes. She looked for the cat to give her comfort. "Motu, Motu where are you? Tch, tch, tch, kitty, come here…"

Instead of Motu, it was Hari who appeared by the dividing wall. Radha was following him. "Your cat was here this morning," he said. "But I don't know where he is now."

"Why are you crying?" Radha piped up. "Have you hurt yourself?"

Anjali shook her head. Her heart was so full of her troubles that she couldn't help telling the Over There children all about them. She gulped down her tears.

"My story is full of mistakes. I know it is! It takes me ages to write anything. I can't remember my spellings and I hate school."

Hari was quite used to comforting his own sister, and he had a kind heart. "Maybe I could help you," he offered.

"How?"

"I don't know yet," admitted Hari. "But I could try. I'm not bad at writing stories. Why don't you bring your books and show me what you're doing in class?"

"It's too dark now," said Anjali.

It was clear to Hari that she wasn't convinced. She probably thought it would be a waste of time, but he didn't give up. "How about at break time tomorrow, in school?"

Anjali slowly nodded.

So, the next day, Hari looked at Anjali's written work.

"Hmm… It could be a lot better. But I'm sure you're not stupid – your sister told me you tell good stories."

"Would you like to hear my favourite one? It's called 'The Ghost in the Guava Tree'."

"Go on then," Hari agreed.

It was a really scary story, and the way Anjali told it made Hari realise that Seema was right – her sister had imagination and real talent.

Anjali had just got to the bit where the ghost shakes down the guava fruit before it's ripe, when the bell rang and she had to stop.

"Same time tomorrow?" asked Hari.

It quickly got round the village that Hari was washing Brother Angelo's car, and doing an excellent job, so Fernando from the bicycle hire came to see him. He had made a lot of money from his business by charging tourists 100 rupees to rent out a bike for half a day. With the profits he had bought himself a small car that took him and his old mother to market on Mondays.

"Will you take on a contract to wash my car on Sundays? We go to church, so it's a good time to do it. I'll pay you the going rate."

Hari liked the sound of the word "contract". It was so business-like. Within a week, he had another three customers all wanting their cars washed: the doctor, another teacher from school and the man who ran the local taxi service.

At the end of the month, Hari gave his mother 200 rupees to go towards the project of building up capital. He did some quick mental arithmetic and calculated that it would take 15 years for him to make enough money to set up a shop for his family. It wasn't good enough! He would have to find a better way.

Hari stared out to sea. Monsoon clouds were rolling in – soon no one would want their cars washed because the rain would do it anyway. Fifteen years. By then Hari would be 30! A grown man, who shaved and went to work, and might even be married with children. Perhaps he wouldn't be living in the village any more. Maybe he'd have a big job somewhere in Margao. Maybe he'd even have a car or motorbike of his own. But in the meantime there was the immediate problem of bills. Two hundred rupees might sound like a lot of money, but he knew he couldn't always depend on getting it. In any case, there were so many expenses – food and clothes, medicines for when someone was ill, *and* the amount they owed the grocer.

The whole time, Anjali had been making up new stories and Hari had written them down for her.

"They're your stories, but if you copy my writing, exactly as I've written it, at least your teacher will be able to read them."

Hari wrote clearly and carefully so Anjali could follow his example and her teacher was amazed that she could now read her stories. Anjali's writing wasn't good, but it was better than before. Most of the s's faced the right way, the d's weren't back to front and the g's even had tails! Soon Anjali began to get good marks and even her test results showed an improvement, which made her much happier. She began to like going to school, now she could show her teacher that she wasn't stupid or lazy.

When Madhu told his wife and mother that Anjali had got 60 out of 100 for her essay, Amma said, "It's the Them Over There boy. He helps her. They are quite good friends."

"What's that fellow after?" Madhu asked suspiciously, and Amma replied that she thought he just had a good heart.

A few weeks later, something woke Hari before dawn. He didn't know what time it was, but his ears caught the cock crowing down the lane. There was no moon, but enough light to see a little. He leaned out of the window to breathe the fresh, early air.

What was that? He saw a dark shape moving slowly through Next Door's yard. He heard the latch click in the gate. Someone was heading for the beach! Nimbly, Hari jumped out of the window and headed in the same direction.

At first, he couldn't see anything; but, as it grew lighter, bit by bit, he made out a figure standing on the edge of the water.

The water swirled and eddied round the person's feet, but the sea was backing away with the tide going out.

Then he saw that it was Amma. She was bending down to take water in her cupped hands and lifting them above her head. She opened her fingers, letting the water splash over her face and head. Hari thought she might be praying to the ocean. Or maybe she was doing a spell. Her actions were slow and regular.

Amma turned round, so Hari hid himself as best he could by sitting down behind a big rock. The old lady stumbled about in the wet sand, peering here and there, as though she was looking for something. She picked up a piece of driftwood and flung it into the waves. She gazed out to sea.

CHAPTER FIVE

Amma was becoming more and more forgetful. She was starting to wander out by herself, sometimes at night and sometimes at dawn. Here she was now on the shore stumbling along, picking up debris from last night's tide, muttering and even laughing to herself. Maybe she was thinking about the past, because she seemed to be lost in her own world.

Then she started off down the beach, taking the same way that she and her granddaughters went in the evenings.

She walked fast, with her sari tucked between her legs, like all fisherwomen. She was old and bent, but still wiry and strong.

The fishing boats were just visible out at sea. In an hour or so they would be back with their catch. But it was still very early, and there was no one about on the beach.

Hari followed some way behind. He was curious, but also a little worried. Old people sometimes behaved in strange ways. Maybe Amma was doing what she used to do when she was young.

Then she would have walked along the shore to gather brushwood from the forest, and carried home a huge load balanced on her head.

Hari watched as she scuttled along like a hermit crab until she got to the edge of the creek. Then she started to cross the water that flowed into the sea. The forest was on the other side. Here the water was shallow, but there was a small patch of quicksand in one place. Amma went forward, one cautious step at a time. Now she was up to her knees in water. Suddenly, she seemed to lose her balance.

From where he was, Hari could see that she wasn't getting to her feet again. He saw her arms thrashing about as she tried to regain her balance. He began to run...

As he got closer, Hari saw that Amma was in trouble. She was stuck in the patch of quicksand. The mud was up to her shins, and she was shouting, "Help! Help!"

"Coming, Amma!"

Hari looked around, his heart beating fast. He needed a pole, or a long piece of wood. It was no use offering his arm because then he would be sucked in, too. He couldn't see any driftwood lying around, so he doubled back and ran to their fishing boat. In the bottom of the boat was a stout bamboo pole, which was used to hold up the sail. He grabbed it, ran back and held it out for Amma.

The old lady was very frightened now. Tears were running down her cheeks and her breath came in sobs. She took hold of the bamboo pole. Hari could see her using all the strength in her arms to heave herself up. He tried to guide her to the firm part of the bank. The mud was as thick as treacle.

Very slowly, Amma's toes managed to find a grip, and then her feet. Hari began to pull her gently towards him. It took a good few minutes until she was safe and sound.

When Amma finally gained dry ground, she was covered in black mud from head to toe. She was out of breath, but grinning her toothless grin. She looked down at herself, shook her head and started to cackle with laughter. Hari was so relieved that she was all right that he started to laugh, too. Arm in arm, and laughing together, they walked slowly back home in the beautiful sunrise.

"Good boy. You saved the old lady."

Hari noticed that his dad didn't call her the Witch, but old lady.

"Well done, son." His mother gave him a hug.

At school, Hari discovered that the news had travelled fast. Lots of children came and patted him on the back.

"Hero!" they whispered.

In assembly, Brother Angelo called him to the front and the whole school clapped.

"My brave car washer!" Brother Angelo beamed. "Come to my office. I have something to tell you."

Hari couldn't help wondering what he'd done wrong. But he didn't need to worry.

"I've been hearing reports about you," Brother Angelo said, beaming at Hari from behind his desk. "Good things."

Hari felt himself go all hot.

"I hear you have spent a lot of time helping Anjali with her work. And her teacher says her writing is getting better. If she really is writing those stories, she can't be stupid, can she? They show a lot of thought and intelligence. So much so that I think she may be dyslexic. We are going to send her to Margao to be properly examined by a special teacher. No one in this school knows how to deal with dyslexia. We are only a little village school."

"But," he went on, "we are not so little that we cannot reward bravery and kindness. I have some extra money in the school funds for scholarships. I am going to pay for your schooling until you finish your studies. That should help your parents. Well, what do you think?"

Hari was standing with his mouth open. He closed it quickly and then opened it again to thank Brother Angelo. School fees and books taken care of! What would his parents say?

When Radha and Hari came home from school they found their mother in a very good mood.

"Our neighbours – Madhu, his wife, Tara, Anjali, Seema and Amma – have sent you some sweets."

The sweets were sticky and fresh from the sweet shop. There was syrupy jalebi and rich almond barfi. They couldn't remember the last time they had eaten anything like that!

Motu squeezed himself between them to get his share from Radha. She lifted him on to her lap and cried, "What's this, Motu? What do you have around your neck?"

Motu was wearing a collar made out of a piece of cloth. It felt heavy and made a jingly noise.

Radha untied the cloth. It was stitched like a long bag and there was something hard inside it. She tipped it out and shouted, "Mother, look at this! Motu has brought us a gold necklace!"

It was a heavy golden chain with tiny medallions. The design was old fashioned, like the village women used to wear when they got married.

Hari took it in his hand and felt its weight. "This is worth a fortune!"

"We must take it back to our neighbours," their mother said.

"Oh, Mum, if it's worth so much then it could be our capital!" cried Radha, thinking of her dream of opening a shop.

At that moment, a shadow fell across the doorway. Amma was standing there, spick and span in a new sari. Her face was shining and her hair was freshly oiled.

"Can I come in?"

It was the first time anyone from Next Door had crossed their threshold for many, many years.

Mother fetched a stool and Amma sat down.

"We were just going to bring this back to you. Motu was wearing this bag with a gold necklace round his neck. It must be yours, I think?"

"Yes, it is mine," replied Amma with a twinkle. "Actually," she hesitated a little, "I sent it over for Hari, to say thank you. First he saved our cat, then he helped

Anjali and now this morning he saved my life! Who will he save next?" She started cackling, showing all her gums.

They all joined in.

"What are you going to do with my gold chain, Hari?"

"He's going to open a shop!" shouted Radha. "Now we have capital, don't we, Hari?"

"Is that right, Hari?" Amma turned to him.

"Yes, Amma. After we have made some good profit, we could buy an outboard motor and dinghy like Uncle Madhu, then Papa and I can go fishing in the deep."

Mother had just finished making a glass of hot, sweet tea for Amma, when the three girls from Next Door put their heads shyly round the door.

"Come in and share our sweets," she said.

The girls daintily took a small piece of barfi each.

Radha and Seema quickly joined hands and went out to play a game of Knuckles. Hari and Anjali got busy with a book. Amma and Mother started to catch up on generations of silence. Only Tara sat there, prim and proper in her best frock. She had powdered her face, ready for her evening walk.

"Let's all go to the creek together," suggested Amma after a while.

"Thank you, Amma," said Hari's mother, "but I have so much work to do.

You go and enjoy yourselves, but try not to fall into the quicksand!"

Amma got to her feet, cackling all the time. She took Seema with one hand and Radha with the other. The other three children followed her as she led the way, a little bent, but still strong and wiry, across the sands of Bamba Beach. As she walked, she hummed a tune.

"I know!" Anjali said. "Let's sing! I have just made up a new song:

Now we are friends
This is how it ends
One, two, three, four
Who could ask for any more?"

READING ZONE!

QUIZ TIME

Can you remember the answers to these questions?

• Why are there fewer fish in Bamba Bay than there used to be?

• What is Anjali really good at?

• How much did Hari give to his mother at the end of his first month of washing cars?

• What did Hari save Amma from?

• What did Motu the cat have tied around his neck?

READING ZONE!

WHAT DO YOU THINK?

The author describes the characters in detail, including their personalities, likes and dislikes.

Can you make a list of each of the characters and write descriptive words to show what they are like? Do any of the characters remind you of someone you know?

READING ZONE!

GET CREATIVE

Hari does three good deeds and is rewarded with a scholarship.

Can you write a short newspaper report about what Hari did, and how he was rewarded? Try to use quotes from the book to help you add detail.

You could also draw a picture of Hari to go in your report.

READING ZONE!

STORYTELLING TOOLKIT

The book has lots of description of the setting, which is in Bamba Bay in Goa, India.

Draw a table with two columns. In one column, list things in the book that aren't often seen in the UK, e.g. coconut trees. In the other, things that are commonly found in the UK, e.g. homework.

This is a good way to plan settings for your own stories.

Look out for more books in the
BLOOMSBURY READERS SERIES

MACBETH

RETOLD BY
TONY BRADMAN

BLOOMSBURY

9781472987862

Lightning flashes and thunder rolls. Macbeth
is riding home from battle when he meets
three strange old women who tell him
he will become king. Which is impossible...
unless Macbeth is prepared to kill.